The Witches of
Creaky-Cranky Castle

The Witches of Creaky-Cranky Castle

Victoria Whitehead

Illustrated by Jan Smith

ORCHARD BOOKS

ORCHARD BOOKS
96 Leonard Street, London EC2A 4RH
Orchard Books Australia
14 Mars Road, Lane Cove, NSW 2066
ISBN 1 85213 284 1 (hardback)
ISBN 1 85213 606 5 (paperback)
First published in Great Britain 1991
First paperback publication 1994
Text © Victoria Whitehead 1991
Illustrations © Jan Smith 1991

A CIP catalogue record for this book is
available from the British Library.

Printed in Great Britain by
The Guernsey Press; C.I.

☆ ☆ ☆ Contents ☆ ☆ ☆

☆ ☆ ☆ I ☆ ☆ ☆

The Letter

LIVING WITH TWO WITCHES AND A WARDLE WAS ALL VERY WELL BUT IT SEEMED LIKE WEEKS SINCE Trina had left her family. In the Real World, of course, it was only the twinkling of an eye. Mum and Dad were away in Hong Kong and Uncle Barney had come to stay at Trina's house to look after the shop and the dog and Mrs Halliwell had come to look after the children. The shop was local and oriental crafts, the dog was Buster and the children were Trina and Jamie.

If Mum and Dad had not gone away and

left her behind, then Trina would probably not have gone away either. But I wouldn't want you to misunderstand me. It was not that she did not have a good time. Living in a castle with two witches, dozens of cats, hundreds of mice and a wardle was sometimes hairy, sometimes scary, sometimes funny, but never dull.

It was the letter that did it ... the one that had her name and address on it, beautifully printed and showing through a window in an envelope.

Mum said that she should throw it away because it was junk mail, and Dad said the same.

But Trina did not throw her letter away. When Jamie came in through the front door, after playing Junior Scrabble with Jack, his friend, next door, Buster made him welcome by flinging himself at him like an all-in wrestler. Trina ran to meet him.

"Look at my letter," she sang happily. "It's from two witches and a wardle. It says, I've been *chosen*. I'm one of a small number of lucky children to be invited to enter a competition."

"Sounds like rubbish to me," Jamie said, playfully fighting Buster off. "R.U.B.B.I.S.H." (He liked to spell words out for emphasis.)

"It's not rubbish," Trina insisted. "The witches are called Bellawhistle and Milliewart and they're making me an 'unmissable introductory offer'." She was reading now.

Jamie brushed past Trina and burst ravenously in through the kitchen door—where he knew there was a frozen cream and chocolate gateau defrosting on the table. He had persuaded Mum to take it out of the freezer an hour before.

"Let's see," Jamie said, grabbing at the letter. His interest had been awakened by the mention of a competition. He liked competitions and often won them.

"I'll do it for you, if you like," he volunteered. "I'm much better at them than you."

Trina knew that he was right. She was the one who was good at making up stories and he was the one who was good at working out puzzles, but she clutched her letter to her. It had *her* name on the front, not *his*.

"No, thank you," she said proudly. "I'm going to do this one myself."

"O.K.," Jamie said, shrugging, "if that's what you want. It's all right with me."

Trina pounded upstairs with her letter. This was *her* competition. If she did it right, *she* would be the winner.

Downstairs, in the kitchen, Jamie sat down at the table. He took his glasses off to clean them.

"A competition in a letter sent by witches and a wardle?" he said to Buster. "You know, my sister gets loonier every day."

☆ ☆ ☆ 2 ☆ ☆ ☆

The Brilliant Plan

BUT TRINA WAS NOT LOONY. WHAT JAMIE DID NOT KNOW AT THAT TIME, AND WHAT TRINA did not know either, was that the two witch-sisters, called Bellawhistle and Milliewart, who had sent the letter to Trina had magicked her name and address out of a witch's hat along with many others. Trina's full name was Katrina Abbott. It had come out on top of the list.

The reason they had written to Trina was this. One night, several days earlier, they had been disturbed by a crashing sound, so loud that it shook the foundations of their castle (Creaky-Cranky Castle, it was called) and shaken them out of bed. Bellawhistle and Milliewart had rushed out of their bedrooms screeching.

"What happened?"

"What is it?"

"What was that crash?"

"It seemed to come from the castle roof!"

The wardle, a brown, furry, very handsome, long-toed creature who lived with the witches, had come skedaddling down from the castle battlements, where he liked to spend his nights.

"Whelp! We've been belliwogged!" he cried.

"Calm down, wardle!" Bellawhistle had croaked in her loudest, calmest croak. (It sounded like twenty frogs.) "Tell us what has happened."

"The Darkful Dreadella has cannoned us!"

"The Darkful Dreadella?" echoed Millie-wart. Her voice was like a cockerel's and it went up high as she spoke. "Oh no, Bella-whistle, my sister, my badger. He means the dreadful Darkella! Oh, what can she have been up to now?"

Bellawhistle and Milliewart followed the excited little wardle up a winding staircase to the castle roof. There they found an enormous jagged hole.

"Darkella's really done it this time," rasped Bellawhistle, "shooting welliboggs from her cannon again, I expect. When will that woman ever stop? When will she ever leave us alone?" and she huffily adjusted her raggedy black cloak over her nightie.

"Who does she think she is?" cried Millie-wart in indignation. "Shooting her monsters all over the countryside, just to prove she's the best!"

"Hole in the hoof," grunted the wardle.

"What are we going to do now about the whacking great mole in the hoof?" He was always getting the letters mixed up in his words.

They ran back in to the castle and into the room immediately below the battlements. There they found a stinking monster-wellibogg, lying in a heap beneath the hole. He belonged to Lady Darkella of Sharkersfastle and it had been his turn, this time, to be shot from the Sharkersfastle cannon. He was not as fierce or slimy as some of Darkella's monsters (who were sometimes called boggs for short) but he was quite bad enough. He was rubbing his bottom with his great clawed hand and groaning pitifully. He had a huge muscular tail and two scaly heads. He was wearing two round yellow crash helmets. Written on one, in bright red letters, was "Sharkersfastle Castle". On the other one in smaller letters was "the castle with the best

magic in the Witchland Woodland world".

Darkella was one of those witches who always had to do things better than anyone else and let everyone know it.

The witches and the wardle angrily sent the stinking monsterwellibogg cannonball home, with a sharply worded letter pasted to the top of his left-hand helmet. Then they all sat down together on the balcony outside the room beneath the battlements. All witches' castles in the Witchworld have wardles to do the cooking and the cleaning and other household jobs. This wardle was a special one, however. He did the housework, but he always sat down with the witches to eat and drink as well.

Bellawhistle uncorked a bottle of parsnip pop and they began to discuss what they were going to do about the whacking great hole in the Creaky-Cranky Castle roof. There had been a time when they could have fixed it right away with magic, but not any more. Thanks to Darkella's scheming and Milliewart's silliness, the Karrizzum, which had always been the main source of the Creaky-Cranky Castle magic, no longer had a heart.

"What we need is some roofmenders," crowed Milliewart. "Roofmenders from the Real World."

"What we need is some *money* from the Real World to *pay* some roofmenders," Bellawhistle muttered scratchily.

Milliewart hooted with laughter and an owl somewhere hooted a reply.

"Witches don't have money from the real world!" she scoffed.

"*You* had some money from the real world when you sold the Karrizzum heart," Bellawhistle rasped accusingly and she gave her sister a withering glare.

Milliewart blushed purple.

It had been silly of her to sell the Karrizzum heart. She knew that now. But Darkella had come round for tea one afternoon and, on the same day, a travelling salesman had called at Creaky-Cranky Castle, looking for interesting things to buy. Darkella had put a beam-zapper spell on Milliewart, and it made the fat little witch's head go funny. She did not know what she was doing for a bit and when she came to her senses, she found that she had had sold the Karrizzum heart to the travelling salesman. He had said that it would make a very pretty paperweight for someone in the Real World. Milliewart had spent the money the travelling salesman had given her on a magnificent wide-brimmed hat covered in cherries and daisies. When she found out what Darkella had made Milliewart do, Bellawhistle was so furious that she hung from the ceiling, spinning like a top for a week.

The wardle, who had been sitting quietly on the rail of the balcony while the witches argued, grunted and looked at his parsnip pop. He was feeling a buzzing sensation in his head and that usually meant either the pop was off or he was getting a brilliant idea.

"I've got a pabulous flan," he announced. He meant that he had a fabulous plan.

The witchsisters stopped bickering and looked at the wardle dourly.

"A terrible plan, I expect," groused Bella-whistle. "A plan, I expect, that's no good."

She knew he was a clever wardle really and that the plan was probably good. But she never praised him. She did not want him to become conceited.

"We can bake something to smell," said the wardle, "Then we can take money."

"He means something to sell to make money," Milliewart chortled. "Make something to sell? What could *we* make to sell, wardle, you silly old walrus?"

"A wagazine ...." suggested the wardle. "Full of madventures for kids. A bomic ... for children."

"A magazine for children?" Bellawhistle said thoughtfully.

"A comic?" echoed Milliewart.

"Maybe," said Bellawhistle reluctantly. She did not usually like to agree with anything anyone said, but she did think that this might be an idea that *could* possibly work.

The more the witchsisters and the wardle thought about the idea, the better it seemed, but it soon became clear that two witches and a wardle did not know nearly enough about what children like to produce something of that kind, alone. They were going to need help. Help from a child maybe. Help from a child from the Real World.

Together they formed the rest of the plan. The witches decided that the wardle should write one hundred letters to one hundred children, to find out which ones might be interested in helping with the scheme.

"One hundred letters!" protested the wardle, who hated writing letters. "Surely not one lundred."

"Off you go!" Milliewart cried, gaily opening a fresh packet of peppermint toffees and eating three. "The sooner you get started, the sooner you'll be done."

The wardle spent the whole of that night writing just one letter. He used fifty-seven sheets of writing paper and a whole bottle of ink. Bellawhistle was not very pleased when she got up next morning and saw all the blots and spelling mistakes on the final copy.

"This will never do," she cried. "I suppose I'd better make a spell."

"Why didn't you do dat in the first place, you willy fat based stitch?" grumbled the wardle into his plump and fluffy chest, and Bellawhistle tweaked his ear.

The truth was that the Karrizzum could still be used for mild magic. It was powerful enough for small spells. Bellawhistle had to dance around more to make them work, however, and she thought she was too old for all that, so she did not like to make Karrizzu-magic unless she absolutely had to.

The wardle scuttled behind Bellawhistle up the main castle staircase to the huge castle dining room. It was called the great hall. There the wardle hopped up on to the dining table and placed his letter in the middle. Still grumbling, he leapt off the table and scurried to the door, where he waited.

Meanwhile, Bellawhistle went to the far end of the great hall to a carved wooden cabinet. She unlocked it with a key that was hanging on a hook near by. She took out a beautiful pearly glass ball, shot with rainbows and hollow at the centre. That was the Karrizzum without a heart. The old witch shook the magic ball, spat on it and wiped it with her sleeve. Raising it high above her head, she spun in dizzying circles aroung the dining table.

Small spell, magic mild

she sang hoarsely,

> *Letter fit for clever child*
> *Heart lost*
> *Sad day*
> *Strong magic*
> *Went away*
> *Can't be helped*
> *Do our best*
> *Bellawhistle*
> *Use the rest*

She spun even more quickly around the table a second time. When she stopped, she had to wipe the sweat off her brow. Then she leaned over and held the Karrizzum just above the wardle's letter. Uttering a witchy screech that made the wardle's face screw up and his ears turn down, she sang these final words.

Take this splotchy blotchy letter
And turn it in to something better

There was a waft of air through the dining room window. The wardle's fingermarked and crumpled letter curled up then opened like a daisy in the sun. It had been transformed. It was perfect, not a blot or a spelling mistake in sight. It was beautifully printed out on a sheet of crisp, white paper. A brown stamped envelope lay beside it.

Bellawhistle and the wardle looked at each

other and smiled. They were both very pleased with the result.

In the end, this letter was the only one that was written. It was sent to the child whose name had come out on top of the list. Her name was Katrina Abbott and she lived in a house attached to a craft shop in a pretty village, not far from the Witchland Woodland boundary. Trina received that letter with great excitement, the day that Mum and Dad broke the news that they would be going away.

The Competition

WHEN MUM TOLD TRINA ABOUT THE TRIP TO HONG KONG, SAYING THAT BOTH SHE and Dad would be going to buy stock for the shop and that they would be gone for a week, Trina cried buckets. She did not want to be left behind. She used up the last half of a box of tissues and after that she cried on the dog and wet his fur.

If she could not go too, Trina did not want Mum and Dad to go either. Jamie said she was just being silly. He did not mind them going. Mrs Halliwell was nice and she would be coming to stay at the house to look after the children and Uncle Barney was great and he would be coming to look after Buster and the shop.

Mum told Trina that, if she was good, and she helped Mrs Halliwell with the dusting and the cleaning and the cooking, she would have something to keep her busy and then the time would pass more quickly. Trina did not like cleaning or dusting or cooking and she said so loudly and very many times. If only she had been old enough, she thought sadly, to help out in the shop like Jamie—to help out in any way other than housework—then she might not have minded Mum and Dad going away and leaving her behind. In fact, if she had had something, anything else to do, she might not have minded at all.

When Trina opened her letter later on that morning it was the sunniest moment of her week.

CREAKY-CRANKY CASTLE was the address at the top. SOMEWHERE FARAWAY AVENUE it went on, WITCHLAND WOODLAND WORLD, and what the letter said was this:

CONGRATULATIONS! YOU ARE ONE OF THE FEW LUCKY CHILDREN WHO HAVE BEEN CHOSEN TO RECEIVE THIS UN-MISSABLE INTRODUCTORY OFFER. WE ARE GIVING YOU THE OPPORTUNITY TO PURCHASE, AT RIDICULOUSLY LOW COST, THE FIRST IN A SERIES OF WITCH-LAND WOODLAND COMIC MAGAZINES FOR CHILDREN.

FURTHERMORE WE ARE DELIGHTED TO REPORT THAT WE ARE NOW ALSO IN A POSITION TO OFFER YOU AN OPPOR-TUNITY TO ENTER OUR FABULOUS COM-PETITION. THE FIRST PRIZE WILL BE A CHANCE TO VISIT A WITCH'S CASTLE OF

YOUR CHOICE, ABSOLUTELY FREE.
PLEASE RETURN THE ENCLOSED FORM
TOGETHER WITH YOUR COMPETITION
ENTRY AND A NICE ROUND POUND COIN
AS SOON AS YOU POSSIBLY CAN.

WITH THE KINDEST REGARDS,

YOUR FRIENDS,
BELLAWHISTLE, MILLIEWART AND THE
WARDLE

Trina raced upstairs to her room and lost no time in filling in the form. It said,

I AM INTERESTED IN RECEIVING
FURTHER DETAILS OF YOUR SPECIAL
OFFER
SIGNED . . .
and she added her name—TRINA.

The competition was simple. She had to unjumble the following letters:

SAY CRACKETY-CRANKLE

Trina worked on the unjumbling for half
an hour, but could not make sense of it at all,
so she put her pride in her pocket and went
downstairs to join her brother and the dog in
the kitchen. She sat down on a stool and
looked at Jamie who was engrossed in his
magazine. Buster was engrossed in the chocolate gateau that was defrosting on the table.

"SAY CRACKETY-CRANKLE," Trina said.

"What?" said Jamie.

"SAY CRACKETY-CRANKLE," she repeated. "Can you unjumble those letters?" And she pushed the piece of paper with the competition on towards him.

"You said it was *your* competition," Jamie pointed out.

"It *is* my competition," she said. "But you're *so* clever I thought ... "

"It's your competition. Do it by yourself," said Jamie. "Y.O.U.R.S.E.L.F Self!"

He was not usually that mean. It was just that he did not like the way she had not let him help her in the first place.

"I'm going to see if Dad wants a hand," he said, and getting up from the table he went off to join Dad in the dark little stockroom behind the shop. Trina sighed as she heard the stockroom door creak as usual. She wished that she could help Dad out in the shop as well, but Dad always said she chattered too much and only got in the way.

"Creak," said Trina to herself. "Creaky stockroom door. Creaky-Cranky stockroom door. Creaky-Cranky Castle."

Then she had a totally brilliant thought. She raced upstairs to finish the competition.

CREAKY-CRANKY CASTLE

Working backwards she discovered to her delight that the letters of Creaky-Cranky Castle were exactly the same as the letters of SAY CRACKETY-CRANKLE!

She had solved the puzzle! She had done the competition! She had done it by herself!

Thrilled to bits by her efforts, Trina found a pound coin she had stashed away in her drawer. It was two weeks pocket money, waiting to be spent. She stuck it to her competition entry with sticky tape. Then she borrowed a stamp from Mum, who helped her address the envelope. At last Trina ran down the road to pop her competition entry into the fat red letter box at the end of the lane.

When she came back, Buster was in terrible trouble with Mum.

"What's the matter? What's Buster done?" Trina asked.

She did not like it when Mum got cross. Mum did not answer, but Trina saw that Buster had a blob of cream on his nose and a guilty look in his eye. The plate the gateau had been on was empty.

"Never mind, Buster," she said, hugging him hard. "Everybody does silly things sometimes."

When Bellawhistle, Milliewart and the wardle received Trina's competition entry, they were over the moon. Bellawhistle uncorked a bottle of dandelion and burdock pop and put it into three glasses which they clanked together in a toast of celebration.

Milliewart threw the pound coin into a brass coal scuttle that they had put in the middle of the dining table in the great hall, exactly for that purpose. Bellawhistle and the wardle clapped. They knew that one pound was not very much, but soon they expected to have a child staying with them at the castle; one who would help them with the next part of the money-making scheme ... the next part of the fabulous plan.

☆ ☆ ✫ 4 ✫ ☆ ☆

The Prize

IT WAS THE DAY MUM AND DAD WERE DUE TO LEAVE FOR HONG KONG. UNCLE BARNEY AND MRS Halliwell would be arriving at lunch time. Trina still did not want Mum and Dad to go but she felt better when an envelope arrived in the post. It had her name and address on the front. She tore it open. There was another of those beautifully printed letters inside. This one said:

DEAR TRINA,

CONGRATULATIONS! WE ARE VERY DELIGHTED TO TELL YOU THAT YOU

ARE THE WINNER OF OUR COMPETITION. YOU HAVE WON A GUIDED TOUR OF OUR CASTLE AND A CHANCE TO BE THE GUEST OF HONOUR AT OUR GRAND AWARD CEREMONY. PLEASE COME TO CREAKY-CRANKY CASTLE AT THREE O'CLOCK ON REAL WORLD TUESDAY.

WE ARE SENDING YOU A MAP AND INSTRUCTIONS TO SHOW YOU HOW TO GET TO CREAKY CRANKY CROSSROADS. SOMEONE WILL BE AT THE CROSSROADS TO MEET YOU AT A QUARTER TO THREE. THAT SOMEONE WILL BE SHORT AND FURRY AND VERY VERY HANDSOME. HE WILL GUIDE YOU THE LAST PART OF THE WAY TO CREAKY-CRANKY CASTLE.

SEE YOU TUESDAY.

YOUR FRIENDS,

BELLAWHISTLE, MILLIEWART AND THE WARDLE

"I've won the competition, I've won the competition!"

Trina ran wildly up the stairs, shouting at the top of her voice.

Buster was on his way downstairs and there was a collision. Both Buster and Trina landed in a heap at the bottom. Trina set off up again, two stairs at a time and still shouting in triumph.

"I'm invited to the witch's castle on Tuesday! I've won! I've won! I've won!"

Mum was finishing packing in the bedroom. Trina ran in to her.

"I've won the prize. It's a trip to the witch's castle. I *can* go on Tuesday, can't I? Please say that I can go."

"Tuesday! Don't be so daft, Trina. Dad and I will be away by then," Mum said, laughing. "When we come back, perhaps. When one of us can come with you."

"But it's a grand award ceremony," Trina protested. "Let me go. Jamie can come with me if he wants."

"You must be joking," Jamie cried as he walked past the door. "I'll be playing football with Jack."

"But I've won a prize. I've never won a prize before," Trina said sadly. She threw her arms around Mum's waist. "Please Mum," she whispered in her sweetest and most hopeful voice.

"I don't think so, love," said Mum, hugging her. "I'm sorry, but it may not be safe. Wait till Dad or I can come as well."

Trina had to accept that, for the time being at least, the answer was a final and definite no.

That evening, when Mum and Dad had gone, Trina wrote this letter.

Dear Bellawhistle, Milliewart and the wardle,

I'm afraid that I shall not be able to come to the witch's castle on Tuesday. My Mum and Dad have gone away and Mrs Halliwell and Uncle Barney have come to look after me and my brother and the shop. Can I come to the castle with my Mum and Dad in about two weeks time?

With best wishes
from your friend, Trina.

She posted the letter and soon received this one back.

Dear Trina,

We would very much like you to come to the castle on Tuesday. Will your Uncle Barney come with you instead?

With best wishes
from
your friends,
Bellawhistle, Milliewart and the wardle.

☆ ☆ ☆ 5 ☆ ☆ ☆

Uncle Barney

OLD BARNEY BIGGLESWADE LIVED IN THE SAME VILLAGE AS TRINA. EVERYBODY KNEW HIM as Uncle Barney and most people liked him because he was always ready to help out. Sometimes he mended people's roofs. Sometimes he dug their gardens over for them. When Dad had mentioned to him that he and Mum were going to be away for a week, Uncle Barney had been only too ready to come and look after the shop.

Some people said that Uncle Barney was a funny old josser and was probably all mixed up with witches and wizards and the Witch-land Woodland World. They said that he knew things that other grown-up people did not know. But Mum and Dad trusted him and said that they did not mind what he knew or who he knew as long as he looked after the shop properly.

Mrs Halliwell lived in the village too. She had agreed to come and stay with Trina and Jamie and look after them and cook meals for them. She had said she would cook meals for Uncle Barney too, as long as he did not frighten her or get the children involved in anything magical or strange.

It was early in the morning. Mum and Dad were in Hong Kong. Mrs Halliwell was making the children and Uncle Barney some breakfast in the kitchen. Jamie was out walking with Buster. Trina thought that this was the right time to have a word with Uncle Barney about her letter from the witches. She walked in through the stockroom door and went into the shop where he was preparing for customers. He was dusting some things on the counter, with a soft yellow cloth. Trina breezed in behind him.

"Hello Uncle Barney," she said.

"Hello Trina, love," said Uncle Barney. "Come to help me, have you?"

Trina felt guilty.

"I'm not allowed to help in the shop," she said. "I chatter too much and I only get in the way. But I suppose I *can* help with the dusting."

"Good idea," said Uncle Barney.

He found a bright green feather duster and handed it to her. She began humming and flicking it around. She started with some Hong Kong ducks in the big bow window.

Uncle Barney picked up a round and glassy, blue and purple paperweight. Trina's Dad had bought it from a travelling salesman

several weeks before. Uncle Barney sat down on a ladder stool behind the counter and began polishing the paperweight with his cloth.

"No customers yet," he said, stopping polishing to look at the watch that he kept in his baggy old cardigan pocket. "So there's time for us to chat. What are you going to do this week?"

"Not much," Trina said casually. Then she

hesitated. "Except I'll be visiting a witch's castle."

She flicked a ladybird off the petals of a china rose, then turned her attention to some pottery pigs.

Uncle Barney's face broke into a smile under his white moustache.

"Visiting a witch's castle?" he said. "Now which witch's castle would that be?"

"Creaky-Cranky Castle," Trina told him. "You can come with me, if you like."

Uncle Barney chuckled.

"Creaky-Cranky Castle?" he said and a faraway look misted his eyes. "Oh yes, two witchsisters called Bellawhistle and Milliewart and a very handsome wardle live there, I believe ... "

Uncle Barney broke off suddenly, with a loud exclamation.

"Good gracious!" he cried. "What's going on?"

He dropped the glass ball he was polishing on to the counter. It fell heavily, so heavily in fact, that it smashed a dent in the wood.

"What happened?" Trina asked and she darted across the shop to have a look.

"It's this paperweight," said Uncle Barney. "There's something peculiar about it. If you ask me, it's not a paperweight at all."

"What do you mean?" Trina asked.

"Well," said Uncle Barney, "a minute ago it was moving about in my hand. It was beating. Yes, that's what it was doing. It was beating like a heart!"

Trina took a closer look at the glassy object. It was not beating any more. It was about the size of an egg and coloured blue, with purple deep inside. Even deeper was a strand of liquid silver. She picked it up and held it in both hands. She could see her reflection in it, but it made her face look strange.

"Now I wonder however your Dad came by that," said Uncle Barney, peering over his spectacles to study the object closely. His face appeared in it too. His nose looked very big and his chin looked very small. He tapped it with one finger and then he shook his head.

"You know, Trina love," he said, "I don't think this thing, whatever it is, should be here at all. It's not for selling to people, not like a wooden duck or a pottery pig. It's my guess that someone's lost it. Give it to me. I'm going to put it on a shelf, where it will be safe until it can be returned to where it belongs."

Uncle Barney pulled the ladder stool out from behind the counter and pushed it against a wall. He climbed up on to it and carefully placed the small glass object on a shelf where it could not be seen from below.

"A glass egg, beating like a heart?" he said thoughtfully. "Now would you believe it?"

He beamed at Trina as he climbed down

off the ladder stool and pushed it out of the way.

"Something like that can really set a person's imagination going, can't it?"

"I'm not imagining the witches' letter," Trina told him. "It says I'm the lucky winner of a competition."

"A witches' competition?" repeated Uncle Barney.

"I won it," said Trina. "My prize is a trip to the castle. Will you come with me, Uncle Barney? Mum says I mustn't go alone. You've been invited too."

Uncle Barney quite liked the idea of a trip to a witch's castle, but he did not know whether he ought to say "yes" to Trina or not. He had, after all, promised Mrs Halliwell that he would not involve the children in anything strange or magical. Of course, it could be argued that this was one of the children involving *him*. He glanced at Trina, who was watching him with wide and hopeful eyes.

"Well, run and fetch the witches' letter," he said at last. "I haven't been to the Witchland Woodland world for a bit. Show me the letter and I'll see."

☆ ☆ ☆ 6 ☆ ☆ ☆

The Storm

TUESDAY CAME. UNCLE BARNEY HAD AGREED TO GO WITH TRINA ON HER TRIP TO CREAKY-Cranky Castle. Mrs Halliwell had not liked the idea much, but said that she would let Trina go as long as Uncle Barney promised she would be safe.

"Of course she'll be safe, Mrs H.," Uncle Barney had told her. "With me around, nothing will go wrong."

The weather was very wet ... so wet, in fact that Jamie could not play football with Jack. The game was put off until later. Jamie asked if he and Buster could come to the castle too.

"All right," said Trina. She thought that the more people who saw her being a guest of honour, the better.

It was two fifteen. That was the time when Trina, Jamie and Uncle Barney (and Buster, who was going too) were due to leave. They were all gathered in the hall. The rain began pelting down even harder. Storms of droplets pounded against the front door. Some even sprang up and down like grasshoppers under the gap at the bottom.

Mrs Halliwell, who was looking after the shop for the afternoon, had taken off her apron and was all ready waiting behind the counter. Suddenly she saw two large drops of water fall from the ceiling and plop on to the display of paperweights in front of her. The ploppy rhythm quickened into a steady stream of water.

She ran into the hall.

"Stop!" she cried in a panic. "Uncle Barney, stop! There's a leak above the counter. You'll have to do something to fix it!"

Uncle Barney was not very pleased because he did not want to be late for the meeting at the crossroads. Quickly he went to the garage to find a ladder and climbed up on to the roof of the shop to see where the water was coming through. He found a hole and had to go and fetch some tools to mend it.

He sloshed through the storm, to and fro, fetching and carrying and hammering and climbing and mending. At last the hole was fixed and he sloshed back into the shop again.

"Well, how's that?" Uncle Barney said wiping his face on his sleeve. "Is that better, Mrs H?"

Mrs Halliwell checked that no more water was dripping on to the counter.

"That'll do for now," she said. "Yes, thank you, Barney but you'd better be getting yourself and the children off now quickly. I don't want them to be late."

At last Jamie, Trina, Buster and Uncle Barney set off on their trip to the Creaky-

Cranky crossroads. The awful thing was that by now, of course, they were horribly, hopelessly late. Three o'clock, the meeting time, had already been and gone. Trina was worried that it might be too late to go at all.

☆ ☆ ☆ 7 ☆ ☆ ☆

Creaky-Cranky Crossroads

BY THE TIME THEY WERE OUT OF THE VILLAGE, THE RAIN HAD ALMOST STOPPED. ONE COUNTRY lane led to another. Uncle Barney drove on between scattered trees, through woods and finally out into the open again. He kept peering at the map that the wardle had drawn and which was now spread out across Jamie's knees.

At last they arrived at a misty crossroads, where four narrow twisting lanes met. The place felt lonely and mysterious.

"This is it," said Uncle Barney, stopping

his battered old car with a jolt. "This is the crossroads where something small and furry and very very handsome should be waiting for us."

As the car engine quietened, everybody looked out of the windows to see what they could see. There was not a soul about.

A damp earth smell rose up to meet them as

they climbed out of the car. Around their feet, they could see that dozens of tiny brown mushrooms had popped up in the wet grass. Buster bounded off to poke his head down as many rabbit holes as he could find. Uncle Barney and Jamie went over to the signpost at the middle of the crossroads to look at what was written there.

The signpost was in a dreadful rickety state. One arm was almost completely missing. CREAK was all it said. It could have been the beginning of CREAKY-CRANKY CASTLE, of course, but who could say for sure?

Another arm was so damaged that only a few letters of the name could be seen. That one said RE ANY ALE or rather -RE--- --AN-Y -A--LE.

"It might be something to do with a pub," Jamie suggested, "or, if you fill the blanks in with other letters, that arm of the signpost could say CREAKY-CRANKY CASTLE too."

The third arm of the signpost had a picture of a castle and a witch on it.

"That arm points to a witch's castle without a doubt," said Uncle Barney. "But it doesn't say which one. Anyway, I doubt we'll be able to get anywhere in the Witchland Woodland World without a guide and a spot of witch's magic."

The fourth arm of the signpost simply said HOME and it pointed back in the direction from which they had come.

Trina stood beside the car, feeling still and unusually quiet.

A soft misty wetness hung around the signpost and the trees and the distant hills. The same mist hung around Trina's shoulders like a cloak. Suddenly she knew with absolute certainty the exact direction of Creaky-Cranky Castle.

"The castle's that way," she shouted to Uncle Barney and Jamie, but they were talking and they did not hear. Trina decided at that moment to go a little way down the track. It wound away from the clearing, through some bushes and off between some trees.

A moment later, Jamie and Uncle Barney came to a decision themselves.

"We're going to choose a direction to go by tossing a coin, Trina love!" Uncle Barney called.

"Where *is* Trina?" said Jamie, looking around.

Trina was nowhere to be seen.

"TRINA, WHERE ARE YOU?" shouted Jamie, but his cry was swallowed by silence.

Everything at the crossroads seemed to be eerily, airily still.

A shiver ran down Jamie's spine.

"Trina, where are you?" he said again, "W.H.E.R.E. are you?"

☆ ☆ ☆ **8** ☆ ☆ ☆

The Wardle

WHAT HAD HAPPENED TO
TRINA WAS THIS.

SHE HAD SET OFF DOWN THAT
little path by herself. She had not intended to
go far, just the first few yards. As the brambles and the undergrowth grew thinner in
front of her they thickened up behind her.
Before she knew it, she had come out of the
bushes and was crossing a brook by a small
wooden bridge. That was where she came
across the wardle.

The wardle had been waiting for Trina for
very many Witchworld hours (Witchworld

time is not the same as the Real World). He had given up hope of the guest of honour ever arriving at the crossroads and had wandered off to gaze morosely into the water under the bridge. When Trina went walking past him with a cheery "hello", he got a terrible fright. He couldn't stop himself from leaping up on to the bridge rail and very nearly falling off again into the icy stream.

"You are whooo?" he growled in deep indignation.

"Trina," said Trina. "Is this the way to Creaky-Cranky Castle?"

"Trina—the Hest of Gonner?" he exclaimed and he spun right around on the rail and was left swinging like a satchel on a hook.

"Slubberputz!!" he said, looking up at Trina. "Well, help me up! and I'll get you to the quastle . . . kick!"

Trina helped him back on to the bridge.

"I'm sorry I'm so late," she said, smiling brightly.

The wardle wiped his ears, which were sagging in the wet, then hopped off the bridge and to a mound of soggy leaves. He burrowed out of the mound a largish package. It was wrapped in black plastic, like the kind that is used to make dustbin bags, and stuck with tape.

"Can we fetch the others?" asked Trina. "They want to come to the castle too."

"What others?" the wardle asked.

"My brother and Uncle Barney," Trina told him.

The wardle looked up at the brightening sky to work out what time it was and thought about how bad-tempered Bellawhistle became if ever he kept her waiting. Sometimes, when she was cross, she tweaked his ear.

"No time. The waiters are witching," he said, deciding that enough time had been lost already. "Open this tox and bake out what you see inside."

"What is it?" Trina asked.

"Magic," the wardle told her. "A small spell. Karrizzumagic. But dat will have to do."

Trina was full of excitement as she undid the black plastic and dropped it on to the ground. Inside was a box covered in purple velvet. She carefully lifted the lid and found herself gazing at a milky white ball, about the size of a melon. It looked as though it was made of glass. She glanced at the wardle, who was frowning impatiently.

"Out it take," he urged her. "Out it take and flurry!"

Trina took the glass ball out of the box. It felt surprisingly light as it lay in her hand.

"Hold on to it hard," ordered the wardle urgently. "The rabbit will do the test, I mean the habit will do the pest—no, I mean the magic will do the nest, the nest? THE REST!!"

And as Trina stood holding the magic ball, the Karrizzum as the wardle had called it, the magic began to do the rest as he had promised.

"And Uncle Barney and Jamie?" said Trina

in a wondering whisper as she felt herself lifted as if on a breeze from that bridge and dropped gently, very gently somewhere else.

"I'll smell them, bell them, TELL THEM!" growled the wardle's voice, first from right beside her then from a long way off.

Jamie and Uncle Barney were still standing at the crossroads when the wardle came hopping out of the bushes to explain to them where Trina had gone. Buster ran to greet him and sniffed him, wagging his tail wildly. Then he licked the wardle's face all over.

"Oh slubberputz yuc!!" grunted the wardle in disgust. "A dorrible hog! Don't do dat again."

And he hopped away back to the under-growth as quickly as he could. Uncle Barney, Jamie and Buster followed.

"So you're the wardle who's going to take us to Creaky-Cranky Castle?" said Uncle

Barney, peering down at the wardle where he was crouched behind a blackberry bush.

"Lorry, borry, SORRY, no," said the wardle. "Sorry but you're too late to go."

"Too late!" exclaimed Uncle Barney.

"Where's Trina? Has she gone already?" Jamie asked.

The wardle nodded and sped off again to take cover behind a raspberry bush even further away.

"Loon," he shouted. "Moon, I mean. No, SOON! She'll be back soon!"

"How soon?" Jamie cried. He didn't want to miss his football match.

"Spoon!" repeated the wardle.

"But we have to know she's safe," Uncle Barney protested loudly.

The wardle was scurrying away now, back towards the bridge over the brook.

"Of course she's wafe," he shouted back over his shoulder full of indignation. "Trina's wafe of course at Quirky-Clonky Castle."

Uncle Barney and Jamie had no choice but to settle down amongst the mushrooms under the Creaky-Cranky signpost and wait for Trina's return. As often happens when real people are close to magic, they soon became drowsy and fell asleep. After a while, Buster got tired of chasing rabbits and came and sat beside them. He put his head on Jamie's knee and soon he fell asleep as well.

The Witches

TRINA HAD LEFT THE WOODS WHERE THE DAY HAD BEEN SO WET. SHE HAD ARRIVED, WITH THE help of the Karrizzum, somewhere where a thin veil of cloud masked a dark blue sky and the sun was shining gently. She was standing on a cobblestoned terrace in front of a tall creeper-clad castle. This, of course, was Creaky-Cranky Castle.

Two witches were waiting at the castle entrance at the top of a flight of mossy steps. Fourteen cats sat watching on the steps beside them. One of the witches was wearing a hat

with cherries and daisies on the brim. That
was Milliewart. The other one was wearing a
black witch's hat with the point bent over at
the top. That was Bellawhistle.

"Katrina Abbott, dear?" Bellawhistle

croaked like someone who has laryngitis. Her face was very pale. "You're here at last, I see. Perhaps you would care to explain how your arrival has been so seriously delayed?"

Trina stared at Bellawhistle nervously.

Milliewart stepped forward. She was shorter, fatter and more colourful than Bellawhistle and she had a smile all over her rosy face.

"You're scaring the child, sister," she yodelled. "Better let me take care of this. Better let me speak." She stepped down two of the mossy steps.

"Yoohoo, my duckling," she called to Trina. "Tell us, the dear old witchsisters, why you're so late, and then we can go inside."

"I'm sorry," Trina shouted back, "but it was raining very hard at my house at a quarter past two today and there was a hole in the roof above our shop and Uncle Barney had to get a ladder from the garage to fix it."

Tears of sympathy rose in Milliewart's eyes.

"A hole in the roof?" she cried. "Bless you, my chicken. My sister and I understand absolutely the problems of anybody who suffers with a hole in the roof. You should see the whacking great hole in the Creaky-Cranky Castle roof. It's big enough to fly a wellibogg through."

Bellawhistle kicked her sister's shin.

"ssh!" she hissed crossly.

She did not want the guest of honour to know *all* the castle business.

The smile left Milliewart's face for a moment. Then it returned, but it was not as big.

"Well, enough of this chitchat," she continued, lifting her scarlet skirt to stomp down more of the steps towards Trina. "Now that you're here, come inside and have a peppermint toffee. The award ceremony's finished but the guided tour of the castle is just about to start."

Milliewart was at the bottom of the steps now. She put her arms around Trina and squeezed her, then, taking her by the hand, she led her back to the top.

Bellawhistle was watching the Karrizzum and took it from Trina as quickly as she possibly could.

"How could the wardle leave you with the Karrizzum and no one to guard it," she muttered testily. "And talking of the wardle—where *is* the silly creature?"

"Do a coming spell," suggested Millie-wart. "He won't get back without the Karrizzum." And she took three toffees from her pocket, gave one to Trina and had the other two herself.

"Hmph!" said Bellawhistle grumpily. "You mean, what's left of the Karrizzum," and she looked pointedly at Milliewart, who

grinned self-consciously and chewed hard on her toffees.

"A coming spell for the wardle? Oh all right," Bellawhistle said. "I suppose I better had."

She held the Karrizzum above her head and, lifting her knees up high, she did a dance like a Highland Fling.

> *Wardley hops*

she croaked

> *Witchy hobbles*
> *Whisk the wardle*
> *To the cobbles.*

There was a rumbling noise and a bright flash and suddenly the wardle appeared back amongst them with a grunt and a squeak, which are the usual noises that accompany a wardle moving very quickly from one place to another. Bellawhistle tweaked his ear and made him scowl. Then she looked at him questioningly.

"Well?" she snapped. "Where's Uncle Barney? Don't tell me the child came alone."

"Buncle Arney and Crainy at the joss-roads," the wardle told her. "By now they'll be a peep." (He knew that Jamie and Uncle Barney would have fallen asleep.)

Bellawhistle was disappointed, but she sighed with resignation.

"Well, never mind," she said. "The Real World time is not the same as ours. They'll not be waiting long. At least we have one guest of honour."

Carefully holding the Karrizzum aloft, she bent down and offered Trina her pale and wrinkled cheek. Trina realised to her acute horror that she was supposed to kiss it. That she did, but it made her teeth ache.

"Now, wardle, take the Karrizzum and put it in the Karrizzum cabinet," Bellawhistle ordered, as she straightened up after her kiss. The wardle took the Karrizzum from Bellawhistle, hopped away into the castle and was quickly lost in its darkness.

Bellawhistle and Milliewart walked on either side of Trina to guide her in through the castle entrance. When Trina's eyes became accustomed to the gloom she could see that she was in a lofty hall. A few candles flickered in holders on the walls. A black cat ran across her path and nearly tripped her over. As far as Trina could make out, there was not a soul about apart from the witches, the wardle and the cats. She began to wonder where the award ceremony had been held and where the other guests were, but she did not yet feel she knew anybody well enough to ask. For the moment, at least, she could not find anything to say.

The witches led her through the echoey hall and up a dark and winding staircase. There were spiders living around the stairs and hundreds of mice who ran for cover as the witches approached. Trina thought with delight that this was just as she had always imagined a witch's castle to be. Her bounce returned and her spirits rose as she followed the two sisters up and up and round and round a little spiral staircase.

A quarter of the way upstairs, she found her tongue again and she began to chatter. She told the witches all about her Mum and Dad, the shop, her brother, her dog and Uncle Barney. She was just about to start on Jack and his mother and his hamster when they all arrived at step number forty-four and the witches had to stop climbing, lean against the wall and take a breather.

Trina, who was not tired at all, stood on tiptoe to peep out of a tall narrow window above the step. She could see, from there, the cobblestoned forecourt where she had first arrived. After half a minute or so the witches were ready to start climbing again. There were thirty-three more steps; that made seventy-seven altogether. Trina talked all the way up them, twenty to the dozen.

At last they arrived at a wooden door right at the top of the tower. It led to a perfectly square little room that looked just as if it had come from a fairy tale. There was one window through which the light slanted on

to a narrow bed, with a patchwork quilt laid over it. This window was open and looked out over the castle roof.

Trina stopped talking to gasp with delight.

"Now, now, my turkey," said Milliewart, beaming all over her rosy face, "tell us if you like the room."

"Oh yes," breathed Trina happily.

"Good, then, it's yours," croaked Bellawhistle, "for as long as you'd like to stay."

"Oh, I can't stay," said Trina, "Uncle Barney and Jamie are at the crossroads. They're expecting me back."

"Expecting you back? They should have been here too!" Bellawhistle exclaimed. "But time is not the same in the Real World. They won't have much time to miss you. *You're* here now, and here you'd better stay."

Trina was a bit uncertain. She did not want Jamie and Uncle Barney to worry.

"The wardle has spoken to them. We'll have you back in no time," Milliewart cried. "Don't go away yet. We invited you here because we need your help."

"You need my help?" cried Trina, delighted at the prospect of being useful. Then she hesitated. "You don't want me to do cleaning or cooking, do you?" she asked.

"No, no, no," Milliewart cackled. "No, no, no. Not the cooking or the cleaning, my coot. Of course we don't want you to help us with that. We want *you* to help us with something much more important. We want *you* to help us with the wardle's brilliant plan."

Life at the Castle

SO YOU SEE, THAT'S MORE OR LESS THE WAY IT HAPPENED. THAT'S MORE OR LESS HOW TRINA came to be living in Creaky-Cranky Castle with two witches and a wardle and dozens and dozens of cats. It seemed to Trina as if she had been away for weeks. To Uncle Barney and Jamie the time went in a flash.

Trina was having a truly wonderful time. The witches and the wardle were looking after her very well indeed. She was given a raggedy red spotty dress to wear. The wardle ran it up on the sewing machine and it had a bow at the waist. The witchsisters found her a smart black pointed hat, although she did not wear that much because it got in the way. Each Witchworld day, Trina, the witches and the wardle sat down together at the table in the great hall to work on the first copy of the Creaky-Cranky Castle magazine.

Trina was told eventually the whole story about the hole in the castle roof and the dreadful Darkella, but she was never allowed to meet her. The witchsisters thought that Darkella would probably want to steal Trina if she saw her. Whenever Darkella called at the castle, everyone pretended to be out. Nobody ever told Trina the tale of the missing Karrizzum heart. It was embarassing enough that a castle as famous as Creaky-Cranky had so little magic: nobody wanted Trina to know how silly Milliewart had been.

The first copy of the Witchland magazine was soon finished. It was called *Witches*

Weekly Number One. It was packed full of amazing adventures of monsters and witches and zombies. It also had recipes and cartoons and jokes. Trina loved making up stories and writing them down and Bellawhistle was always ready to help her clear up any spelling mistakes and blots.

Trina's ideas flowed very fast and she chattered constantly. While Trina was around the witchsisters had far less time to bicker. This not only made the witches happier, it made the wardle happier too. He grew very fond of Trina.

A lot of magazines were produced and sent to the Real World newsagents, who sold them to Real World children.

Bellawhistle and Milliewart asked for the money they received from the newsagents to be sent to them in the shape of one pound coins only.

As the money for the magazines arrived back at the castle, the witchsisters poured it into the brass coal scuttle, which was soon filled to the very brim with thick and coppery, clattery, scattery, exchangable, arrangable, non-bendable but spendable, round, sound, grand pound coins.

The witches and Trina and the wardle were thrilled that their scheme had been such a wonderful success. The time was drawing near when Trina would have to be returned to the crossroads. Trina did not really want to go home—she was enjoying herself so much, and it was good to feel that she was being really useful. The witchsisters said that she could have just one more Witchworld night at the castle and then that would have to be the end of her stay.

Unfortunately that was the night when things went very seriously wrong.

☆ ☆ ☆ II ☆ ☆ ☆

Darkella

IT WAS DURING THAT WITCH-WORLD EVENING THAT IT HAP-PENED. TRINA AND THE WITCHES had had their supper (slotti-root soup with mushrooms and dumplings for the witches; fish fingers and peas for Trina) and were getting ready for bed. It was still quite early, but Trina was already on her way up the seventy-seven stairs to her turret bedroom. Bellawhistle and Milliewart were planning an early night too. The wardle never went to bed early. He played out until all hours of the night with the owls and the bats on the battlements. Nobody was expecting anybody to visit and nobody was keeping a lookout.

At stair number forty-four, Trina stopped, as usual, to glance out of the window at the cobblestoned terrace below. As she did so, she heard a loud screeching of brakes and saw a long limousine draw up outside. It was driven by a glum little wardle in a peaked cap. As she watched, a haughty witch, in high-heeled shoes and an enormous hat with flowing scarves—purple, green and black—swathed around it, climbed from the car. She clutched her gleaming, scaly cloak around her and strode towards the front door. Trina had never seen Lady Darkella of Sharkersfastle before, but she thought this surely must be her.

She raced down the narrow turret staircase to warn the witchsisters, but she was too late. Milliewart was already in the entrance hall, opening the door. She was in her rollers and her frilly nightie. When she saw Darkella standing there, she cried out, "Bellawhistle-sister! Oh no! Look who's just arrived!" and she flurried back upstairs to get dressed, leaving Darkella standing on the doorstep.

Trina tried to slip away unnoticed before Darkella saw her, but as she turned to leave she heard Darkella calling from the door-way.

"Hello, child. I've heard so much about you. I'm glad we've met at last. Come here and shake my hand."

Trina turned around.

"Hello," she said shyly, and she began to walk towards the witch.

Bellawhistle arrived downstairs then, all wrapped up in a towel and wearing a shower cap. When she saw Darkella standing there and Trina going towards her, she grabbed hold of Trina's arm and whisked her off up the grand staircase, shouting as she ran.

"Wardle, wardle, come downstairs and attend to Darkella immediately!"

The wardle came down reluctantly from the battlements to usher Darkella inside. Nobody wanted to see her or speak to her, but this time they could not very well say that they were out.

Trina, Bellawhistle and Milliewart all had to get dressed again and go down to the great hall in order to entertain Lady Darkella in the manner to which she was accustomed. The wardle grudgingly prepared some food for the second supper of the evening, then sat down at the end of the dining table, as far from Darkella as possible.

"Well, isn't this cosy?" Darkella said when she, the witchsisters and Trina were all seated at the window end of the table with plates of smoked salmon and lemon wedges in front of them.

She looked Trina up and down as if she was considering buying her in a shop.

"So *this* is the Real World child that all the witches in all the castles around here have been talking about."

Trina thought that Darkella looked like a deep sea fish. She did not like the purple circles around her eyes nor the hook on the end of her nose. She fixed her attention on a lemon wedge, studied it hard and did not speak.

Bellawhistle and Milliewart picked at their smoked salmon and did not speak either. So it was left to Darkella to go on.

"I hear, dear Bellawhistle and Milliewart," she said imperiously, "that you have a scheme in operation. Now why don't you tell me all about it? How has this little slip of a girl managed to make you so much money?"

Still nobody replied.

But the silence felt terrible and eventually Milliewart, who was looking like a red balloon that was about to pop, could restrain herself no longer. She stood up, pushed her chair back, beat on the table three times with her fist and cried out, with more feeling than was wise.

"Listen, Darkella. Listen, you vicious old piranha. It is thanks to you and your schem-

ing ways that we have hardly any magic left. And it is thanks to you and your cannon and your wellibogg, we have been left with a whacking great hole in the Creaky-Cranky Castle roof. We *had* to find a way to make some money."

She sat down hard on her chair, pursed her lips, folded her arms and said, "I'm not telling you any more."

Darkella beamed with satisfaction.

"Yes, of course," she said, "I understand how angry you must be."

As she spoke, she looked Milliewart straight in the eye in a way that made the fat little witch's head spin.

"But come along now," Darkella coaxed, "just tell me how a couple of silly old witch-sisters and a wardle have managed to make so much money. Tell me that and then I'll go away."

"It was a magazine!" Milliewart blurted out. "A magazine and Trina helped us write it!"

Bellawhistle frowned at her sister and reached out under the table to kick her in order to shut her up. But she could not reach her and Milliewart went on,

"We send the magazines to the Real World! We get Real World money back. We're sending for roofmenders soon . . ."

She stopped dead because she was hit in the

eye by a wholemeal bread roll, catapulted across the table from the spikes of Bellawhistle's fork.

"Whoops, sorry, Milliewart, my dearest," Bellawhistle croaked. Of course, she did not mean it.

"The Real World child writes this magazine for you, now, does she?" Darkella said, looking first at Bellawhistle, then at Milliewart, then at Trina. All the time, her eyes were flashing enviously.

"The child can't do anything, Darkella," Bellawhistle said tartly. "She's been no use to us. She talks too much and only gets in the way. You wouldn't want to have her around."

"Of course," Darkella continued, "I have an enormous staff of witches, wardles and two-headed stinking monsterwelliboggs to guard my castle, drive my car and make my meals, but they don't know much about doing repairs. In fact I think it's true to say that they haven't got a toolbox between them. I want some workmen from the Real World too. I'll borrow the child to write a magazine."

She was looking really pleased with herself now.

"*The child must go back to the crossroads*, Darkella," Bellawhistle said.

"No, no, she can come and stay with me instead," Darkella said. "She can sleep in the stables with my stinking monsterwelliboggs."

"Darkella . . . NO!!" Milliewart cried.

"Milliewart, YES!!" Darkella cried even louder, and before anyone knew what was going on she shot a beamzapper from one of her purple fingernails and burnt a sizzling round brown hole in the tablecloth.

Bellawhistle, Milliewart and the wardle all jumped to their feet. Trina wished that her chair would swallow her up. Darkella was using serious magic now, and serious magic would be needed to counteract it.

"I think you had better go home, Darkella, if you're going to behave like that," Millie-wart said in exasperation.

Darkella replied by lifting one hand.

She zapped beams from two more fingernails and made two big holes in the portrait of Bellawhistle's uncle that was hanging on the wall. The portrait fell to the ground and Darkella rose up in the air like a ghost.

Now she was standing on the table and looking twice the size she had before. She kicked aside the lemon wedges and wafted the remains of the smoked salmon into all corners of the room.

Bellawhistle cast the wardle a look that he understood immediately to mean "Get the Karrizzum from the cabinet!". Mild magic

was not enough, but it was all they had.

"I hate it when Darkella does this," Millie-wart muttered to Bellawhistle.

"Calm down, Darkella," said Bellawhistle soothingly, "there's no need to get in a caffuffle . . ."

But Darkella was already in a caffuffle.

The wardle quietly opened the Karrizzum cabinet.

"The plan is mine. The scheme is mine. The child is mine. The castle's mine," muttered Darkella darkly.

"They aren't!" protested Milliewart, and she stamped her foot. "If you don't belt up, Darkella, we shall have to use the Karrizzum against you . . . "

"The Karrizzum!" cried Darkella, laughing. "What? Without its heart?"

And her eyes moved sharply to the cabinet, where the wardle was crouched. He had unlocked the door and was about to take the Karrizzum out.

"STOP, WARDLE!" commanded Darkella. "DO NOT MOVE!" and she aimed a fingernail shot right past him. It zapped against the corner of the Karrizzum cabinet. The door slammed shut, the Karrizzum still inside. The cupboard locked itself. The key fell to the floor. A diagonal crack ripped through the door but did not break it apart.

"There there, Darkers old thing . . . "

Milliewart attempted to speak again, but Darkella used a further shot that spun around the little witch's head and silenced her. That was five shots. Darkella had ten shots in all, one from each fingernail, and after that she could not zap anything more for a while.

The great hall filled with a steamy swirly mist. Everything became wrapped up in it, including the wardle, whose eyes became glazed before he went stiff as a board and fell over backwards. Before anybody could so much as utter the words "Say Crackety Crankle," the entire household had fallen under a spell: it had become enchanted; it was in Queen Darkella's power.

The Prisoners of Creaky-Cranky Castle

GUIDED BY DARKELLA AND HER FINGERNAILS, BELLAWHISTLE AND MILLIEWART ROSE FROM their seats at the dining table and moved, as if in a trance, down into the dungeons. There they locked themselves in a cell. The wardle lay on his back still stiff and did not move.

Trina sat as if she was glued to her chair. She looked at the wicked witch and tried to produce a cheerful smile.

"Shall I go to bed now?" she asked.

That usually went down well at home.

"No," said Darkella, polishing her

zapper nails on her cloak. "You can stay up late if you like. I think I'll take you off to Sharkersfastle right away. You can get started on the magazine first thing in the morning."

"I can't do it on my own," Trina explained. "You see, the witches, the wardle and me did the first one together."

Darkella continued to look at her from eyes like pools of fish oil. Then she looked away and sighed as if Trina was the most troublesome person in the world.

"Oh, very well, she said. "If you *insist* I'll keep you and the witches and the wardle together to work."

Trina began to feel slightly better.

"I won't take you to Sharkersfastle," Darkella continued. "Instead, my wardles and my welliboggs and I shall move in here. We shall all come to stay at Creaky-Cranky Castle!"

Trina's heart sank again with a thump.

"But I must go back to the crossroads ..." she protested.

"No way," Darkella interrupted.

"Then I must send a letter," Trina went on in alarm.

Darkella laughed a short sharp laugh.

"No letters!" she cried. "No crossroads! No nothing! You're staying here until *I* decide it's time for you to go!"

With that, she beamed a zapper from her thumb. It circled around Trina's head, and made her feel drowsy. Trina rose from her chair and walked like a sleep walker up the seventy-seven stairs to the little square room in the turret and bolted the door behind her. She went to bed and slept soundly, and knew nothing more until morning.

By early next Witchworld day, even before the red fingers of dawn had striped the sky, Darkella had brought a large part of her household from Sharkersfastle to Creaky-

Cranky Castle to stay. She had brought a handful of wardles and no less than forty-seven disgusting, slimy, fierce, enormous, scaly, long-tailed, two-headed, stinking monsterwelliboggs. (That, of course, means ninety-four grey and growling monsterwellibogg heads and goodness only knows how many pointed monsterwellibogg teeth.)

Once she had put her monsters on duty everywhere, Darkella sent for Bellawhistle and Milliewart. Two of the boggs brought them up out of the dungeon and sat them down at the table in the great hall. Trina was allowed out of her turret room and the wardle was released from his lying-flat-on-his-back-as-stiff-as-a-board spell to join them. Darkella provided them with pencils and rubbers and heaps and heaps of paper. She stationed seventeen boggs (that meant thirty-four bogg heads) around the table as well, to keep a careful eye on them, to see that they

worked hard on Darkella's magazine and did not try to escape.

"Right," said Darkella, as she prepared to leave the castle and go shopping. "Right, you pathetic, useless no-good workers. Get started on the magazine!"

And with that, she swished her cloak, adjusted her hat and swept out of the room.

The boggs blinked their one hundred and

two wellibogg eyes (three in each head) and growled in their thirty-four monsterwellibogg throats. They sounded like thirty-four lawnmowers. Then they swished their eighteen monsterwellibogg tails (one of them had two tails, poor thing) and then they began staring at the four magazine producers who were all sitting huddled together at the far end of the table. The workers, for their part, screwed up their mouths and sucked their pencils and looked as deep in thought as they possibly could.

When the monsters felt absolutely sure that the workers were too deeply engrossed in the task at hand to think about making an escape, they stopped staring and shut their eyes and fell asleep. It was like being out in a gale when the beasts began to snore. They leaned back in their chairs and opened their mouths and took in great gulps of air, letting it out several seconds later in fierce gusts of stinking wind,

and making the most horrible racket imagin-
able.

"What are we going to do now?" Trina
whispered to the witchsisters and the wardle.
"If only I could somehow send a message to
Jamie and Uncle Barney to tell them what

has happened. If only I could send a letter."

"We want a fabulous plan," said Millie-wart, glancing at the wardle and unwrapping herself a toffee. "We want a brilliant scheme."

She put the toffee in her mouth.

"Yes, wardle," Trina whispered. "Something clever like you thought up before."

"Hmm," croaked Bellawhistle. "A clever scheme from wardle. That'll be the day."

The wardle felt too miserable to think up a plan at that moment. He hated boggs almost as much as he hated Darkella. And he hated Darkella almost as much as he hated the way Bellawhistle never appreciated anything he did.

"The Tarrizzum," he growled with a shrug. "We'll have to try the Tarrizzum."

Bellawhistle sighed with a tuneful wheeze.

"You know the Karrizzum is nowhere near strong enough without its heart!" she snapped, and she tweaked his ear.

"What happened to the Karrizzum heart?" asked Trina. People kept mentioning that it was missing, but no one had told her how that had come about.

"Darkella put a spell on Milliewart and she *sold* it," Bellawhistle told Trina with a scowl, and Milliewart hid her face in her hands.

Trina looked at Milliewart sympathetically.

"Who did you sell it to?" she asked.

"A very nice travelling salesman," Milliewart cried. "A very nice man indeed!"

"And what happened to the heart after that?" Trina asked Bellawhistle.

"We don't know," Bellawhistle said. "That's the whole point. The heart went to the Real World and we don't know what became of it."

Trina's heart was beginning to beat a little faster now. She had a brilliant thought.

"What colour is the heart?" she said breathlessly. "And does it beat?"

"It's coloured blue and purple with a liquid silver thread and yes, it sometimes beats!" Bellawhistle said.

The witchsisters and the wardle were all looking at Trina enquiringly.

"I think I know," gasped Trina, "where the Karrizzum heart ended up. I think it's in my Dad's shop. Uncle Barney put it on a shelf!"

One bogg woke up suddenly then with a start.

"I HOPE YOU'RE WORKING HARD," he roared.

"WORKING HARD," echoed his other head through a yawn.

"Wess. Wess, of course we are," the wardle said.

The wellibogg jumped on to the table and thumped the other sixteen boggs on the heads with his fist, as if they were a drum set. They woke up and cleared their throats. Then they stared at the workers and began listening to what was going on. This meant that there was no more chance to talk.

"All right, then," said Bellawhistle in her bossiest voice. (She *wanted* the monsters to hear this.) "Let's get started on this magazine."

After a very short time, Trina thought of a story they could put in the magazine, and so did Bellawhistle. Milliewart came up with half a joke but could not remember the end. The wardle and Trina drew some pictures. Bellawhistle did a crossword and the wardle made up the clues. Soon they had the makings of an interesting, clever and exciting Witch-world magazine. *Witches Weekly Extra* was what they decided it should be called.

When they had nearly finished and there was just one last space to fill. Bellawhistle said,

"What shall we put in here?"

Trina leant back in her chair and stretched her arms.

"My brother Jamie loves puzzles," she said. "He's very good at competitions. He nearly always wins."

The wardle looked at Trina.

"Your juther, Brainy?" he echoed.

"Yes," said Trina. "My brother, not my juther, but it's true he's very brainy ... just like you."

The wardle lowered his eyes modestly.

Then he began to jig up and down in his seat because an idea had begun to form itself in *his* mind now. All his bad temper dissolved like salt in slotti-root soup. He chuckled and looked around at the boggs, who had fallen asleep again.

"I know what we can do," he said, "how we can get Darkella out of Cleek and Clacky Castle! I've thought of a pilliant blan and a way that we can fuse the wagazine to blue it."

Trina clapped her hands and Milliewart broke into a stifled peal of laughter.

"Well, tell us, then," croaked Bellawhistle. Even she was beginning to sound eager. ("So what," she was beginning to think. "So what if the wardle becomes conceited.")

"Tell us about your plan, wardle, my dearest, tell us about it now."

✰ ✰ ✪ 13 ✪ ✰ ✰

The Puzzle

THE WARDLE'S PLAN WAS TO
PUT A PUZZLE COMPETITION
IN THE LAST SPACE IN THE MAGA-
zine and to put a message in the puzzle
competition answer. If they could not get a
letter to Jamie and Uncle Barney then may be
they could get a magazine to them with a
message in the magazine.

This was the puzzle that Trina, the wardle
and the two witches made up.

FIND THE FOLLOWING PAIRS OF
LETTERS AND READ THE HIDDEN
MESSAGE were the instructions.

My first is in saFEty, help is the aim
My second in wiTCh, Darkella's the name
My third is in wisHBone, the wish
can't be said
My fourth is in LUck if our message is read
My fifth is in steEP castle roof
must be mended
My sixth is in zAPbeam whose power
must be ended
My seventh is found in monstERs all stinking
WElliboggs next, all growling and blinking
My ninth is in bIG. That's the idea to start
My tenth is in brougHT. So please
bring the heart.
My whole is a message. Solve me. Do not
dawdle.

Help!

Love from Trina, the witches and wardle.

The pairs of letters from all the puzzle
words spell FETCHBLUEPAPERWEIGHT.

This can be divided into three words. These are FETCH BLUE PAPERWEIGHT.

When the magazine was ready, dozens of copies were produced and sent to newsagents in the Real World. The more people who saw the magazine in the Real World the better it would be for sales. Darkella said that she wanted the money that came back to be in the shape of delightfully clattery, thick and thumpity, shiny, shimmery, round pound coins and she too, had a brass coal scuttle ready to receive them. She kept it in the middle of the dining table in the great hall. If the first edition of the magazine went well, it was her plan to force her team of workers to produce another and then another. This way she would become even richer than she was already—rich with Real World money!

The wardle was allowed out of Creaky-Cranky Castle only once. He told Darkella that he needed to go out to gather some mushrooms for his slotti-root soup. He said that he knew of a very good place for mushrooms but that he would have to go to the Real World, to a place called Creaky-Cranky crossroads.

Darkella, who loved mushrooms in slotti-root soup, reluctantly agreed to let him go. She insisted, however, that he took two big stinking monsterwelliboggs with him, just in case he took it into his head to deliver any letters to anyone or to try to escape.

Once they had arrived at Creaky-Cranky crossroads, the stinking monsterwelliboggs sat down on top of some thorny blackberry bushes to watch the wardle as he gathered mushrooms. They moved about a bit as they sat there and laughed a lot as well, because they enjoyed the scratchy feeling of the prickles beneath them, but they had twelve eyes between them so they watched the wardle very carefully too.

"Look," said the wardle, hopping across the clearing to the giggling stinking monster-welliboggs, when his basket was about half full. "Look, can you see what I can see? There, under the signpost. There's two peeping sleeple and a hog."

He meant, of course, that there were two sleeping people and a dog.

The welliboggs stopped laughing for a moment and peered over towards the sign-post. There, Buster, Jamie and Uncle Barney were still asleep, still waiting for Trina and still unaware how much time had passed for her in the Witchworld. Not long had passed in the Real World since she had gone away.

"Might as well leave them a wagazine," the wardle suggested casually to the welliboggs. "I just happen to have one here." And he pulled a copy of *Witches Weekly Extra* from under the mushrooms in his basket.

Three of the stinking monsterwellibogg

heads laughed deep in their wellibogg throats and agreed immediately that it was a good idea to leave a copy of the Witchworld magazine for these people. They had heard Lady Darkella say time and again that the more people in the Real World who saw the magazine, the better. But one wellibogg head hesitated. It was not quite so sure.

"Lady Darkella said no letters," he pointed out doubtfully.

"No, hetters. No, of course not. No," cried the wardle. "No nutters, just a wagazine."

With a look of pure innocence all over his face, he handed the magazine to the welliboggs for inspection. All the wellibogg eyes looked through the magazine. Not one saw anything suspicious.

"Shall I leave it den?" said the wardle.

"As you like," said one wellibogg head. That was the one who had been doubtful before.

"Go ahead," said a second. That one had seen nothing wrong with the idea in the first place.

"Seems all right to me," said a third.

"Right ho," said the fourth.

The wardle tried not to show how pleased he was, but he could not stop himself from jigging up and down a bit and he hid a grin in his plump and fluffy chest.

He hopped gaily back across the clearing and slipped the magazine into Jamie's hand.

The welliboggs began to laugh jovially as they frolicked amongst the brambles once again and the wardle gathered mushrooms until his basket was full. At last it was time to go.

"Come on, wardle," said the welliboggs as they wiped away the tears of laughter from their cheeks. "Time's up. Let's be off."

And with that, they climbed to their feet and began to lope away.

Before the wardle followed them he took hold of Jamie's shoulder and shook him gently. Jamie's glasses, which had already become dislodged as he slept, fell to the ground. When Jamie woke up, slightly startled, he opened his eyes and put his glasses back on. By the time he had properly come to his senses, the wardle and the welliboggs had disappeared.

He looked at the magazine, which he was clutching in his hand. It was called *Witches Weekly Extra*. Completely mystified, he began to look through it. When he came to the last page, he stopped. He saw the puzzle and thought it looked interesting. He had a pencil in the back pocket of his jeans. He took the pencil out. In no time, he had solved the puzzle and written down the answer. He wrote it on the edge of the page.

FETCHBLUEPAPERWEIGHT he had written down. He could see quite easily that that could also be FETCH BLUE PAPERWEIGHT. He did not know what it meant, but he saw Trina's name at the end of the puzzle and realised right away that this was some sort of message from her.

Buster was asleep with his head on Jamie's leg. Jamie tugged gently on the dog's ear.

"You know, Buster," he said, "it seems as if Trina's managed to get her name into a magazine with some witches and a wardle. Things around here get loonier every day." Buster snuffled and awoke. He lifted his head, saw some chaffinches squabbling in a tree nearby, jumped to his feet and began to bark. That woke Uncle Barney up.

"Oh dear, oh dear, did I fall asleep?" the old man said as he slowly sat up and yawned.

"Look what I've found, Uncle Barney," Jamie said urgently. "It's a magazine and there's a message in it from Trina. It seems as though she may have got herself into T.R.O.U.B.L.E. Trouble."

Bellawhistle and Milliewart had to stay in the dungeons after they had helped produce the first magazine. That was so they could not get near the Karrizzum. It was just a precaution, because Darkella knew that the Karrizzum magic was not very strong. Twenty welliboggsentries were stationed in the great hall around the dining table to watch the scuttle full of coins.

"Keep an eye on the Karrizzum cabinet while you're in there, will you?" Darkella had said to the welliboggsentries.

"Right ho," they had said and they did, taking it in turns to sleep.

The wardle stayed mainly in the kitchen, cooking. Trina was allowed to wander about Creaky-Cranky Castle, doing odd jobs and generally making herself useful. She fed all the cats twice a day and did a little dusting. She cheerfully ran errands for the wardle and visited Bellawhistle and Milliewart in the dungeon. She sat and chatted to them, or played games with them . . . games like Junior Scrabble, Snakes and Ladders, Ludo, Cluedo, Foodo and Dungeons and Dragons.

It was the sort of day, in the Witchworld,

when it felt as if something big was about to happen. Trina had got up that morning and put her jeans and T-shirt on because it made her think of home. She was sitting on her bed, in her little turret room. The room was full of cats. As she glanced out of the window, past the ears of one of the bigger cats, and into the sunlight, she could see the top rim of a dark cloud climbing up over one of the parapets.

"It's going to rain," she thought.

The sun, still bright above the cloud, was throwing shadows on the tiles. She could make out the shape of a man walking across the roof towards her. As the shape came closer the cloud slid across the sun and Trina could see quite clearly that it was none other than Uncle Barney.

Quick as a flash Trina jumped on the bed, climbed out through the window and ran towards him. She flung her arms around him.

"I'm so glad you came," she cried. "Did you understand the message in the magazine?"

"Yes," he told her. "Jamie and I worked it out together. Once I realised that you wanted me to fetch that strange beating thing we found in the shop and bring it here, everything else fell into place."

"That strange beating thing," Trina said,

"is really the Karrizzum heart. It has most of the Creaky-Cranky Castle magic in it. It was sold by mistake and sent to the Real World and the witches haven't got enough magic and they can't get rid of the dreadful Lady Darkella. She came to stay and brought her stinking monsterwelliboggs and she won't let me come home."

Uncle Barney shook his head as Trina poured out the whole story.

"Oh dear," he said, giving her a hefty hug. "I should never have let you come here on your own."

"I know," said Trina, "and I shouldn't have walked off like that. I know that now."

And she shed a few tears because she was so relieved and she felt so much better now that Uncle Barney had arrived.

She wiped her eyes on her T-shirt.

"So did you bring the Karrizzum heart?" she said.

Uncle Barney put his hand deep into his cardigan pocket. He pulled out the glassy egg-shaped object. Its blue was deeper than ever and its purple richer. The liquid silver was moving about inside, causing the heart to beat. It clearly needed to be back where it belonged.

"Here it is," said Uncle Barney. "With that in my pocket, I had no trouble finding my way from the crossroads. Jamie and Buster are still at the crossroads. Jamie wants to get home in time to play football with Jack."

He put the Karrizzum heart back in his cardigan pocket.

"Now," he said with a look that told Trina he was ready for business, "now that I'm here, tell me what we have to do and hurry. It looks as thought there's a thunderstorm brewing and it's high time I took you home!"

☆ ☆ ☆ 14 ☆ ☆ ☆

The Karrizzum

TRINA HELPED UNCLE BARNEY TO CLIMB THROUGH THE BED-ROOM WINDOW, THEN FOLLOWED herself. She put her head out of the bedroom door to check that there was no one about.

Trina and Uncle Barney knew that they had to be careful because some stinking monsterwelliboggsentries had seen Uncle Barney when he had first arrived at the castle. They had asked him if he was a roofmender and Uncle Barney had thought that he might as well say "yes". The monsterwellibogg-sentries had then, in fact, very politely, shown

Uncle Barney the way up on to the roof. If they now caught him inside the castle, with Trina, they would know that he had not told them the truth and they might well turn fierce and nasty and blow bad breath all over the place. That was a terrible thought.

Trina led Uncle Barney quietly, quickly and stealthily, down the seventy-seven stairs of her turret and out into the entrance hall. Fortunately there was no one about. Next, they crept cautiously down another dark staircase and into the kitchen. The wardle had a chef's hat and apron on and was standing on a stool, stirring some slotti-root and mushroom soup in a cauldron.

When Trina and Uncle Barney came in, Trina said, "Wardle, here's Uncle Barney!"

The wardle swung round, grunted with surprise and whistled between his teeth. That meant that he was pleased. He stopped stirring the soup and jumped off the stool.

"The harrizzum cart?" he gasped. "Did you bring it?"

"I certainly did," said Uncle Barney, beaming.

There was a loud fizzling sound as the soup bubbled up to the top of the cauldron and overflowed on to the stove.

"Slubberputz!" exclaimed the wardle.

He hopped across the kitchen to move it to one side, wipe up the mess and turn down the flame. Within seconds, he had worked out the next part of the plan. He told Trina and Uncle Barney what they would have to do.

Trina would need a feather duster (she chose a green one from the cupboard) and Uncle Barney would need some carpenter's tools. There were some under the kitchen table. Once they had those things, the two of them made, as fast as they could, for the dining room, up the main staircase, four storeys up. The wardle would stir his soup for another ten minutes, then he would leave it to simmer and follow on behind.

Trina walked into the great hall with Uncle Barney. As they entered, twenty monster-welliboggsentries rose to their feet.

"Excuse me, captain," said Trina to the most important head of the most important boggsentry. He had a long sword swinging at his scaly side and his tail was swishing ominously. He had just woken up from a very scary dream.

"Excuse me, but this roofmender" (and she took hold of Uncle Barney's hand and drew him forward) "has agreed to mend the door of the Karrizzum cabinet while he's here. It split when Lady Darkella slammed it with her fingernails the night she first arrived. The Karrizzum isn't safe in a cupboard with a split in the door. That's what Darkella says, anyway."

The boggsentry captain's two heads both looked at Uncle Barney, who was holding out his carpenter's tools to show them.

"All right," said one.

"Right," said the other.

"You may pass," said the first.

All the other boggsentries formed themselves in to a corridor so that Uncle Barney could walk through. When he reached the cabinet, he knelt down beside it and examined the crack in the door.

"I shall need a key," he said.

One of the boggsentries took the key from its hook and handed it to Uncle Barney, who opened the cabinet door and looked inside.

He could not help gasping when he saw the Karrizzum—a bright globe of milky glass shot with rainbows. Turning his back so that the boggsentry guards could not see what was going on, Uncle Barney hastily took the heart from his pocket and popped it inside the Karrizzum. When he had done that the Karrizzum glowed magnificently. Uncle Barney then took a screwdriver and a hammer out of the carpenter's toolbox and, with a great deal of banging, turned his attention to the cabinet door.

Trina, meanwhile, was explaining to the boggsentry captain that Darkella had told her

to dust the Karrizzum while the cabinet was being repaired. She waved her green feather duster at him and he allowed her past. Through the sentry corridor she walked. On reaching the cabinet, she stooped down. Uncle Barney moved back while she lifted the Karrizzum out. She carried it very carefully across to the table.

The squadron of scaly guards stood in a

row behind her and each used one of his heads to watch her every move.

The wardle had come up from the kitchen. He was waiting for the right moment to put the next part of his plan into action. When Trina had the Karrizzum in her hands, he knew that the right moment had arrived. Scuttling across the great hall under everyone's noses, he shouted at the top of his voice,

"Right, Triny!" and took a flying leap on to the dining table. "Blow the Karrizzum here! Rawdle's weady!" he cried. (He meant that he was ready.)

Before a single monsterwelliboggsentry could make a single move, Trina had swept up the ball from the table and hurled it across the room. It landed slap bang between the wardle's wiry fingers.

"Tanks Triny!" the wardle cried and as he did so he leapt off the table with the agility of a monkey. Then, cradling the Karrizzum under one arm, he swung across the chairs and came to rest on the wide windowsill.

Poised as he was and clutching the Karrizzum, the wardle was in a perfect position to grab the curtain and swing out on to the thick creepers on the castle wall. He would easily be able to climb down those and on to the ground, but, before doing that, he turned back to face the room. Lifting the Karrizzum above his head he cried, "SNEEZE!"

What he had meant to say was "FREEZE", but it did not come out that way. When he said "sneeze", that was what everybody did.

The air was filled with the sound of "wash-oooooo!" and "paaahhh!" and "harraaah!".

"No, not sneeze. I don't mean sneeze," said the wardle worriedly. "What I mean is . . . is . . . I mean is . . . ."

He screwed up his face until he practically swallowed his ears and with the greatest effort of concentration he had ever mustered in his

life, he shouted, "What I mean is FREEZE!"

The Karrizzum glowed brightly above his head and everybody within earshot did freeze. With a great shudder Uncle Barney, Trina and all the boggsentries crisped up, caked in icicles.

The wardle knew he could not afford to muck up the next instruction. He practised in his head first.

"Esk ... esk ... esk ...." he said to himself. "Monkey, monkey, monkey, no I mean APE...." Then, when he thought and hoped that he was ready, he yelled, "ESCMUMKY! No, not escmunky, I mean ESCAPE!!!"

The instruction worked a treat.

Uncle Barney and Trina thawed immediately and ran amongst the still frozen bogg-sentries and out through the door. They hurtled along the corridor, down the main staircase, into the grand entrance hall, then straight out through the great oak double doors which led to the steps which descended to the cobbled forecourt. The wardle was already there, armed with the Karrizzum and standing with an expression of great self-satisfaction on his face.

The Release

"**W**ARDLE, YOU'RE SO CLEVER!" TRINA EX-CLAIMED.

That was three times she had said it. This time she said it while the wardle had the complete Karrizzum in his hand, and the result was very strange indeed.

He lifted the Karrizzum high above his head and cried out in the loudest voice he had.

Opal rainbowed
Smoothly pearled
Powerglobe from the
Witchland World

Magic heart-filled
Ball of peace
Witches from their cell
Release!!!!

The amazing thing was that, although the words were difficult ones to say, the wardle said them without any problem at all. They came out completely muddle-free. All he had needed was for someone to tell him, often enough, that he had done well.

There was a sound like trumpets playing and choirs singing and some flashing lights and puffs of smoke and Bellawhistle and Milliewart joined Trina, Uncle Barney and the wardle on the castle forecourt. There were sparks shooting out of their ears and their hair was standing on end as if they had had an electric shock.

"I told you not to put CRACKETY CRANKLE on the Scrabble board, Millie-

wart," Bellawhistle was croaking crossly. "I told you something violent would happen."

Milliewart was looking around her in delight.

"Oh shut up Bellawhistle, you weasel," she said. "We're free. Can't you see? We're out of the dungeon. We're free."

Trina began to explain to the witches how they came to be there. The wardle joined in and so did Uncle Barney. Everyone was talking at the same time and nobody noticed that the black cloud that had begun to rise over the castle roof earlier was now standing like an anvil above them. There was a flash of fork lightning that shot into the balcony of the top room of the castle, just beneath the battlements. This was followed by a resounding roll of thunder.

"WHAT DO YOU THINK YOU ARE DOING?"

Darkella's operatic voice could be heard as the clap of thunder rumbled to an end. She was standing on the balcony where the lightning had struck.

Trina, Uncle Barney, the wardle and the witchsisters all stopped talking and looked up with a gasp.

"Oh slubberputz!" exclaimed the wardle.

Milliewart stepped pertly forward.

"We wondered when you were going to turn up, Darkers you old shark," she called out, her voice like a cockerel's, "But you're too late now. We've got the Karrizzum and the Karrizzum's got a heart!"

Even though Darkella was a long way up, her hands could be seen to light up and sharp beams flashed from her long and purple fingernails.

"MILLIEWART, SHUT UP!" she cried, and Millie found herself at the receiving end of one of Darkella's beamzapper shots again. She fell silent immediately.

"Give me the Karrizzum, wardle," Bellawhistle demanded urgently. She did not take her eyes off Darkella. The wardle passed her the Karrizzum. She grasped it in both hands and held it high in the air.

I use the Karrizzum,
she began, croaking loudly like thirty frogs,
To clear the castle
Of unwanted guests
Queens and monsters
Perpetual pests

There was another verse to go but Bella-whistle's spell was rudely interrupted by a furious zipping sound.

Darkella had let rip another beamzapper blast, aimed towards the place where the five were standing. The streak of light hit the ground just at the wardle's feet. He leapt a metre into the air and it shot beneath him. He was so pleased with himself that he could not resist the urge to stick out his tongue and wiggle his fingers on his nose and go "bleh bleh!". That made Darkella so furious that she shot three more beams directly at him. The wardle managed to dodge the beams by dancing like a Spanish dancer. Three, four, five, six, seven, eight beams flashed across the forecourt then two more extra powerful ones from her thumbs. Ten was all that Darkella had. For the time being, she could not zap any more. Her fingers needed time to regain their power.

Darkella stepped backwards on to the balcony to wait. Bellawhistle now had time to use the Karrizzum.

I use the Karrizzum to clear …
she began again. But now, attracted by the noise of thunder and zapping, twenty-six of Darkella's stinking monsterwelliboggs gathered in a fierce circle around Trina, Uncle Barney, the witches and the wardle. They

were all sneering and leering and swishing their tails, not to mention breathing heavily and letting out great clouds of stinking air. They would not, however, advance without a word from Darkella. She was still a long way up on the balcony, waiting for her fingernails to regenerate.

"What shall we do, Darkella, Your Ladyship?" roared one of the heads of an especially enthusiastic bogg. "What shall we do with these people?"

"Never mind the people. Take the Karrizzum!" Darkella instructed from above.

"Right ho," said the monster. "Come on, lads. Last one forward's a creep!"

But the wardle was not having any of this. With a quick glance at Bellawhistle to make sure it was all right to use the Karrizzum power, he grunted, squeaked and shouted "NO! DON'T COME! STINKING MONSTERWELLIBOGGS FREEZE!".

He said it beautifully. The monsters all hardened immediately into solid blocks of ice. They looked like stone creatures in a pleasure park. It would take them several hours to thaw. The witches would be able to have decided what to do with them by then.

Just when Trina, the witches, the wardle and Uncle Barney thought they had dealt with everybody, a last stinking monsterwellibogg, who had been playing patience in the study, and had not heard anything because he had been so engrossed, came loping out to the courtyard. He thought it was time for his tea. When he saw what was going on—that Darkella was on the balcony all zapped out and the other monsters were frozen blocks of ice—he thought perhaps he would go back to his game of patience and miss out on tea for once.

As he tried to sneak away, one of the ears on one of his heads heard Bellawhistle saying to Trina and Uncle Barney and the wardle, "Now we are the ones with the power, my dears, what shall we do with Darkella?"

At that moment, the stinking monster-wellibogg had such a good idea that he simply could not leave without sharing it with anybody. One of his heads called out,

"Shoot Darkella through the roof! She's been doing that to us poor boggs for weeks! Show her what it's like!"

Trina, Bellawhistle, Uncle Barney and the wardle all turned to look at him. Milliewart, who was still under a spell, stared straight ahead. The monster had two huge and toothy grins all over both his faces.

"What did you say?" croaked Bellawhistle in a voice that sounded like fifty frogs.

"He said that you should shoot Darkella through the roof," said Trina.

"Well I won't," said Bellawhistle. Then, several seconds later, "Shall I do that then?"

"I think it's a very good idea," said Trina. Uncle Barney and the wardle nodded.

The walls of Creaky-Cranky Castle echoed. "Good idea. Good idea. What a good idea."

Bellawhistle shrugged.

"All right," she said.

Without more ado, she released Milliewart from Darkella's spell and explained what she was about to do. Milliewart hooted with laughter.

"Here goes," said Bellawhistle.

Both sisters stood with their hands on the Karrizzum and started to chant together.

Darkella, Darkella, your stay here is finished
Your dominance ended
Your power diminished
Your smoked salmon's swallowed
Your magazine's done
Darkella, Darkella, Darkella,
Be gone!

Nothing happened immediately, but there was another flash of lightning somewhere near and a loud rumble of thunder.

Darkella, Darkella, the castle's a mess
Your welliboggs causing the utmost distress
Be shot through the roof,
Oh horrible one.
Darkella, Darkella, Darkella
Be gone!!!!

the witches sang on. Still nothing happened. The stormcloud above had spread to become a dark grey blanket, stifling the sky.

Darkella, Darkella, here's our last verse
For us it's the best, for you it's the worst,
Leave us and let us form schemes on our own,
You scarper off
Back to the wellibogg zone

No longer
Our castle
Will be put upon.
Darkella, Darkella, Darkella
Be gone!!!

A great rush of air howled around the cobbled forecourt. It forced its way in through the castle door and roared up the stair to the topmost room beneath the battlements.

Darkella, standing on the balcony, screamed as she was sucked backwards into

the room. The wind changed and Darkella was lifted first, then catapulted up through the whacking great hole in the castle roof. The storm broke. The rain began cascading down. Darkella disappeared into the sky. She sailed away, turning slowly round and round.

"My power is the greatest! I am the best!" she cried.

It did not seem like it then.

Within seconds, Darkella had arrived back at her own castle. Released by the wind, she dropped like a stone through the Sharkersfastle roof. Because she was so angry and burning still with spell energy, she made a much bigger hole in her own castle roof than the one in the roof of Creaky-Cranky Castle. It was a bigger and a better hole, so you'd have thought she would have been pleased, wouldn't you? But she wasn't. Lady Darkella was never satisfied with anything.

She felt so disappointed with the failure of all her plans that she stayed out of everybody's way for a very long time.

☆ ☆ ☆ 16 ☆ ☆ ☆

The End

THE WORST OF THE STORM HAD COME AND GONE. IT WAS TIME FOR TRINA AND UNCLE BARNEY to cross the Witchland boundary, and re-enter Real World time and the Real World. Uncle Barney offered to return to help the witches repair the hole in the castle roof, but they said that now the Karrizzum heart had been restored they thought they could manage it themselves. Farewells and thanks were exchanged. Trina had to kiss Bellawhistle's cheek and be squeezed tightly by Milliewart. The witchsisters then began to chant another spell.

Witches, wardles spells in songs
they sang as they spun and danced around the Karrizzum.

> *Trina back where she belongs*
> *Uncle Barney beating hearts*
> *End up back where magic starts*
> *Wardle, wardle*
> *Take them to*
> *The crossroads*
> *And then say*
> *Adieu.*

When Trina, Uncle Barney and the wardle arrived back on the bridge near the crossroads a bank of grey clouds could be seen disappearing behind the trees. The sun was shining warmly on the brook and raindrops were glistening everywhere.

Some distance away, Jamie was sitting

flicking through his copy of *Witches Weekly Extra* for the second time. Buster was sitting beside him, awake and alert, his tongue lolling out as usual.

"Here we are! We're back!" Trina cried as she ran out from the overgrown path she had first ventured down only a short time before.

Buster ran to meet her, yelping with joy. Trina hugged and stroked him, burying her face in his fur. Uncle Barney emerged next.

"All right, Jamie?" he said. "Haven't been too long, have we?"

Jamie scrambled to his feet.

"No," he replied. "I'll be in time for the match." He grinned at Trina.

He was pleased to see her back safely, but he did not think it was necessary to tell her, so he just said, "That puzzle you put in the magazine was s.i.m.p.l.e. Simple."

"I know," said Trina, laughing. "I knew it would be easy for you. You're so *clever*."

She hugged him while Buster was greeting Uncle Barney. Last of all came the wardle hopping out from between some brambles. He wanted to see Uncle Barney and Trina safely back in the car so that he could be quite sure that all his brilliant plans had worked out right in the end.

When Buster saw the wardle, he turned from Uncle Barney, jumped high in the air and made a dive for the little creature, barking, wagging his tail and generally going barmy. This was much too much for the wardle.

"Oh slubberputz!" he grunted. "Dorrible hog. I'm off."

He scooted back to the brambles as fast as

his long-toed feet would carry him.

"Goodbye," he called over his shoulder. "Come back some time. Come back soon to see the wardle and the witches of Creaky-Cranky Castle!"

Trina, Jamie, Buster and Uncle Barney all piled into the battered old car. Uncle Barney started the engine and they set off down the narrow winding country lane, the one that the signpost showed would lead to HOME.